KEVIN

Based on *The Railway Se*

Illustrations by
Robin Davies **and** *Jerry Smith*

EGMONT

EGMONT

We bring stories to life

First published in Great Britain 2010
by Egmont UK Limited
239 Kensington High Street, London W8 6SA

Thomas the Tank Engine & Friends™

CREATED BY BRITT ALLCROFT

Based on the Railway Series by the Reverend W Awdry
© 2010 Gullane (Thomas) LLC. A HIT Entertainment company.
Thomas the Tank Engine & Friends and Thomas & Friends are trademarks of Gullane (Thomas) Limited.
Thomas the Tank Engine & Friends and Design is Reg. U.S. Pat. & Tm. Off.

HiT entertainment

ISBN 978 1 4052 5113 6
3 5 7 9 10 8 6 4
Printed in Italy

FSC

Mixed Sources
Product group from well-managed
forests and other controlled sources

Cert no. TT-COC-002332
www.fsc.org
© 1996 Forest Stewardship Council

Egmont is passionate about helping to preserve the world's remaining ancient forests.
We only use paper from legal and sustainable forest sources.

This book is made from paper certified by the Forestry Stewardship Council (FSC),
an organisation dedicated to promoting responsible management of forest resources.
For more information on the FSC, please visit www.fsc.org. To learn more about
Egmont's sustainable paper policy, please visit www.egmont.co.uk/ethical

TO THE TRAINS →

This is a story about Kevin, a little crane who helps Victor mend engines at the Sodor Steamworks. Clumsy Kevin had a lot to learn, but when Spencer ran into trouble, could Kevin come to his rescue?

Early one morning, all was quiet at the Sodor Steamworks. Victor the little tank engine and Kevin the small yellow crane were fast asleep.

Then suddenly, "Poop! Poop! Poop!" – the noise of an engine whistling loudly woke them up.

"Trembling tracks!" said Kevin, as a train rushed by. "What's that noise?"

"That's Spencer's whistle," replied Victor. "I'd know that snooty sound anywhere!"

Spencer was visiting from the Mainland. He wanted everyone to know he had arrived on Sodor.

Victor and Kevin got ready to start the day's jobs. They liked helping broken-down engines get back on their wheels again.

"Let's get to work, Kevin," said Victor, busily.

"Yes, boss," yawned Kevin. He wheeled sleepily to a corner of the Works. But he wasn't watching what he was doing and dropped some engine parts. They landed with a CLANG!

Victor shut his eyes. "Kevin! Slowly, slowly!"

"Sorry, boss," said Kevin. "It was a slip of the hook!"

Meanwhile, Spencer had steamed to Tidmouth Sheds. The engines were still dozing inside.

"Poop! Poop!" whistled Spencer. "Wake up, lazybones! Why don't you get to work like me?" he went on, rudely.

"Poop, poop, yourself!" grumbled Gordon, crossly. He was tired from pulling the Big Express.

"You could do with a wash down," teased Spencer. "Look how shiny my silver paint is."

This made Gordon even crosser!

"You're too big for your buffers," Thomas puffed.

Thomas' crew lit his fire and Thomas built up steam. He shunted slowly out of the Sheds. His first stop would be the Steamworks so that Victor could mend a crack in his funnel.

Spencer steamed after him. "Let's have a race to see who's faster," he said.

"No thanks, Spencer," said Thomas. He knew he had to get his funnel fixed so that he could be a Really Useful Engine again.

"Scaredy-engine!" Spencer sneered.

At the Works, Kevin was still making mistakes.

"Those hooks can be slippy," said Victor, kindly. "Keep going, Kevin."

Just then, Thomas puffed in with Spencer. Kevin was so excited to see them that he wheeled straight into a heap of scrap iron. CLANG! CRASH!

"Hello, Spencer!" smiled Kevin. "Do you need a helping hook?"

"No, I do not! Big engines like me *never* break down," Spencer sneered.

Kevin wanted to show how strong he was, but he hooked too much at once. The load was so heavy, it slipped from Kevin's hook . . . and landed right in front of Spencer! CLANG! CRASH! BANG!

"YOU CLUMSY CRANE! STOP . . . THAT . . . DIN!" shouted Spencer, as loudly as he could.

"Haven't you got a job to do, Spencer?" said Victor, when the noise had stopped. "You're taking up a lot of track!"

Spencer was shocked! He slid out of the Works without saying a word. *No one speaks to me like that*, he thought to himself.

As Spencer puffed away, there was Gordon, pulling the Express.

"Poop! Poop! Hello, Spencer!" whistled Gordon. "How do you like my Express train?"

But when Spencer tried to call back, no sound would come out of his whistle – Spencer had lost his voice! He slid away as fast as his wheels would carry him.

"He's dreadfully rude!" Gordon grumbled to his Driver.

Spencer steamed to Great Waterton to collect the Duke and Duchess of Boxford.

When he reached the station, The Fat Controller and Lady Hatt were waiting there, too.

"Hello, Spencer," The Fat Controller boomed.

But Spencer said nothing.

The Duke and Duchess got into Spencer's coach and Spencer steamed away again.

That night, when Spencer puffed into the Sheds, Gordon was telling the engines how rude Spencer had been that day.

"He needs to learn some manners!" said James.

But Spencer still said nothing.

Thomas was surprised. He thought that Spencer would be sorry for being rude.

Spencer went to sleep feeling very worried.

The next morning, Spencer was still worried. His funnel felt funny and he still couldn't speak. He knew that he couldn't go to the Steamworks to be mended, because he had been unkind to Kevin.

He set off to collect the Duke and Duchess. He had to take them to the Docks in time for their ferry. He took the track that ran behind the Steamworks.

Spencer was going along nicely until, suddenly, he stopped with a splutter. Now Spencer had run out of water, too!

When Spencer tried to whistle, all that came out was a funny muffled sound.

Luckily for Spencer, Kevin heard the funny whistle. He wheeled behind the Works to see what was making the noise. He was surprised to see Spencer, broken down!

"Don't worry, Spencer," said Kevin, kindly. "We can fix you!"

Spencer had never been more pleased to see Kevin. He smiled at the little crane.

Kevin gave Spencer a nice long drink of water, while Victor mended Spencer's whistle.

Then Kevin finished his jobs carefully. He tidied trucks and moved metal – without a single clang!

Soon, Spencer felt much better. "Thank you," he said to Kevin and Victor. "I'm sorry I was rude."

He collected the Duke and Duchess and arrived at the Docks just in time for the ferry.

Kevin and Spencer are now great friends. Spencer always visits Kevin whenever he comes to Sodor – and he *never* shouts.

Two Great Offers for Thomas Fans!

THOMAS & FRIENDS

In every Thomas Story Library book like this one,
you will find a special token. Collect the tokens and claim
exclusive Thomas goodies:

offer 1

Collect 6 tokens and we'll send you a **poster** and a **bookmark** for only **£1.**
(to cover P&P)

Reply Card for Thomas Goodies!

1 Yes, please send me a **Thomas poster and bookmark.**
I have enclosed **6 tokens plus a £1 coin** to cover P&P. ☐

2 Yes, please send me a **Thomas book bag.**
I have enclosed **12 tokens plus £2** to cover P&P. ☐

Simply fill in your details below and send them to:
Thomas Offers, PO BOX 715, Horsham, RH12 5WG

Fan's Name: ....

Address: ....

....

.... Date of Birth: ....

Email: ....

Name of parent/guardian: ....

Signature of parent/guardian: ....

Please allow 28 days for delivery. Offer is only available while stocks last. We reserve the right to change the terms of this offer at any time and we offer a 14 day money back guarantee. This does not affect your statutory rights. Offer applies to UK only. The cost applies to Postage and Packaging (P&P).

We may occasionally wish to send you information about other Egmont children's books but if you would rather we didn't please tick here ☐